The Lonely Pumpkin

Written by
Julia Zheng

Illustrated by
Elizabeth Guch | Gri.seli

D1158714

The Lonely Pumpkin

This is a work of fiction. Names, characters, places, and incidents either are the product of the author's imagination or are used fictitiously. Any resemblance to actual persons, living or dead, events, or locales is entirely coincidental.

Copyright © 2021 Qinghong Zheng
All rights reserved. No part of this publication may be reproduced in whole or in part, or stored in a retrieval system, or transmitted in any form or by any means, electronic, mechanical, photocopying, recording, or otherwise without written permission of the publisher/author.

First printing edition, 2021
Library of Congress Control Number: 2021918793
ISBN: 978-1-7375146-2-6 (pbk)

Printed in the United States of America

This book is dedicated to my mother,
Yanlan, and my sister, Xiaoli, who have
always loved me for who I am.

Mr. Golden picks up a big pumpkin.

It's for trick-or-treating tomorrow evening.

He's going to make a jack-o'-lantern for his dear son, Alan.

Mr. Golden asks Alan, "What face do you want the pumpkin to have?"

"A friendly one, perhaps," Alan replies.

"But it's for Halloween," Mr. Golden reminds him. "I think making it scary is better."

When everyone is asleep, the carved pumpkin comes to life.

He finds himself all alone and decides to look for a friend.

When he sees a spider, he rolls toward him.

"Will you be my friend?" asks the pumpkin.

"No," says the spider. "You look quite scary! I'm a little afraid."

The lonely pumpkin keeps rolling until he meets a cat in a window.

"Will you be my friend?" asks the pumpkin.

"No," says the cat. "You look very angry. It makes me worry!"

The lonely pumpkin leaves the house and keeps rolling.

Under a tree, he meets a bat.

"Will you be my friend?" asks the pumpkin.

"No," says the bat. "You look evil. I don't think I'd be comfortable!"

In a graveyard, the lonely pumpkin meets a skeleton.

"Will you be my friend?" asks the pumpkin.

"No," says the skeleton. "You look too grumpy. I prefer someone friendly!"

On a hill, the lonely pumpkin meets a ghost.

"Will you be my friend?" asks the pumpkin.

"No," says the ghost. "You look like trouble. I don't want the bother!"

In some woods, the lonely pumpkin meets a vampire.

"Will you be my friend?" asks the pumpkin.

"No," says the vampire. "You look awfully mad! I don't think it's a good idea."

The lonely pumpkin keeps rolling until he meets a witch.

"Will you be my friend?" he asks.

"Maybe," says the witch, "if you give me a good reason."

"'I'm a lonely pumpkin. Everyone is scared of me, but what they see isn't the real me. My heart is soft and sweet," the pumpkin says sadly.

"You poor thing!" says the witch. "I could give you a smile if you wish."

"That would be lovely, but my only wish is to have a true friend that accepts me for who I am!"

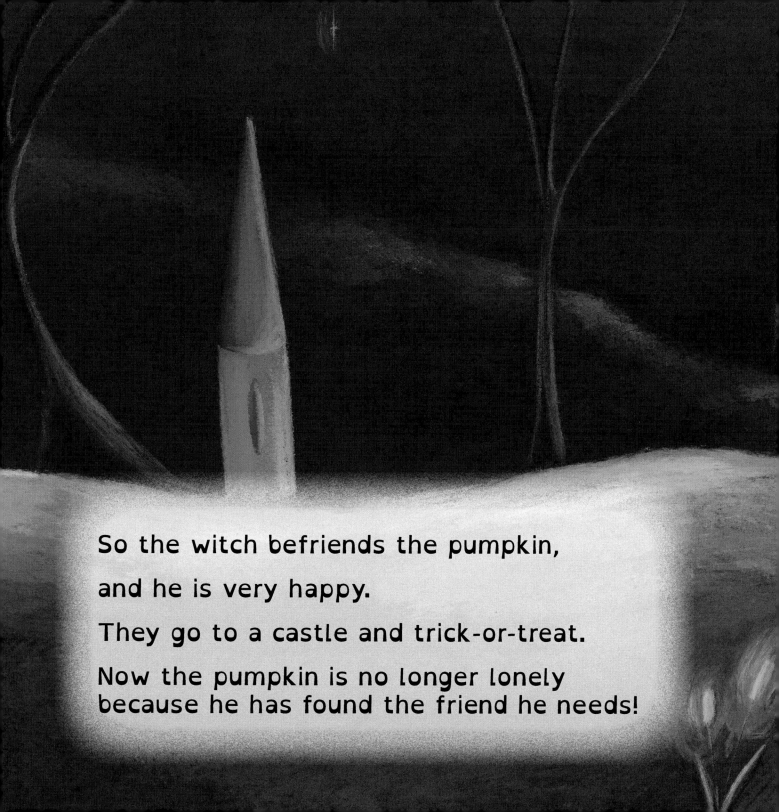

So the witch befriends the pumpkin,

and he is very happy.

They go to a castle and trick-or-treat.

Now the pumpkin is no longer lonely
because he has found the friend he needs!

About the Author

Julia Zheng is a children's author from Fujian, China. She now lives in Massachusetts. Zheng graduated from Nanchang University, where she majored in English and studied Western culture. She taught English in a primary school in southern China before moving to the United States. Her teaching experience and passion  for writing have inspired her to write children's books, especially stories that convey important messages through humor, warmth, and a happy or unexpected ending.

For more books by Julia Zheng, please visit her Amazon Author Page:

https://www.amazon.com/author/juliazheng

Other books by Julia Zheng available on Amazon.com:

The Tallest Christmas Tree
Written by Julia Zheng
Illustrated by Anjali Raj

Thank You
Written by Julia Zheng
Illustrated by (Troika) Maria Novoseltseva

Written by Julia Zheng
Illustrated by Aashay Utkarsh
The Baking Witch

A HALLOWEEN INTERVIEW
Written by Julia Zheng
Illustrated by Eugenia Ard

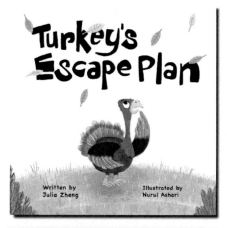

Turkey's Escape Plan
Written by Julia Zheng
Illustrated by Nurul Ashari

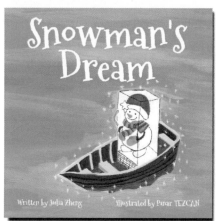

Snowman's Dream
Written by Julia Zheng
Illustrated by Pınar TEZCAN

The Christmas Unicorns
Written by Julia Zheng
Illustrated by Ulia Panfilova

WRITTEN BY JULIA ZHENG
ILLUSTRATED BY GRAZIELLA MILIGI
THE GIVING SNOWMAN

Boo's Halloween Walk

Made in the USA
Monee, IL
18 October 2022

16145162R00017

A sweet pumpkin gets picked up from the farm and carved into a scary jack-o'-lantern for trick or treating. The night before Halloween, he comes alive and decides to look for a friend. However, everyone he meets along the way judges him by his appearance and refuses to be his friend. Will there be someone who will accept the way the pumpkin is and be willing to befriend him? Find out in the book *The Lonely Pumpkin.*

ISBN 978-1-7375146-2-6

9 781737 514626

my first

EASTER

baby Easter book

my first words